For Gabe and his big sisters, Mischa and Phoebe
—L.A.

For Harper and Owen
—B.B.H.

Text copyright © 2016 by Linda Ashman
Jacket art and interior illustrations copyright © 2016 by Brooke Boynton Hughes

All rights reserved. Published in the United States by Random House Children's Books,
a division of Penguin Random House LLC, New York.

Random House and the colophon are
registered trademarks of Penguin Random House LLC.

Visit us on the Web! randomhousekids.com

Educators and librarians, for a variety of teaching tools,
visit us at RHTeachersLibrarians.com

Library of Congress Cataloging-in-Publication Data
Ashman, Linda, author.
Henry wants more! / by Linda Ashman ; illustrated by Brooke Boynton Hughes. —
First edition.
pages cm
Summary: Whether spending time with Papa, singing songs with Grandma,
playing games with Lucy, or racing with Charlie, toddler Henry wears his
family out until bedtime, when Mama is the one who wants more.
ISBN 978-0-385-38512-1 (trade) — ISBN 978-0-375-97348-2 (lib. bdg.) —
ISBN 978-0-385-38513-8 (ebook)
[1. Stories in rhyme. 2. Toddlers—Fiction. 3. Family life—Fiction.]
I. Hughes, Brooke Boynton, illustrator. II. Title.
PZ8.3.A775Hen 2016 [E]—dc23 2014047145

Book design by Nicole de las Heras

MANUFACTURED IN MALAYSIA

10 9 8 7 6 5 4 3 2 1

First Edition

Henry Wants
MORE!

by
Linda Ashman

illustrated by
Brooke
Boynton Hughes

Random House 🏠 New York

Papa's lifting Henry high above his head.

Henry's face is joyful.

Papa's face is red.

UP and UP and UP again.

His arms are getting sore.

Papa stops to catch his breath, but Henry hollers:

MORE!

Grandma plays piano—it's Henry's favorite song.

Henry, on her lap, claps and sings along.

She plays it once.

She plays it twice.

She loses count at ten.

Our ears are getting weary, but Henry cheers:

AGAIN!

Lucy plays the piggy game,
tickling Henry's toes.

Then peekaboo and pat-a-cake
and every game she knows.

Itsy-bitsy spider.
Where's your belly?
Who says "ROAR"?

Lucy says, "I've had enough."
Not Henry.
He says:

MORE!

Charlie races Henry up and down the street.

To the tree and back again.

Tree and back.

Repeat.

Charlie starts to tucker out. He slows a bit, and then . . .

he tumbles on the shady lawn, but Henry shouts:

AGAIN!

A song, a spin, a tickled chin,
a ride across the floor;
a race, a chase, a silly face,
and Henry's calling:

MORE!

Henry's in his jammies now.
The sun's been set awhile.
He gathers up some bedtime books
and stacks them in a pile.

Mama says, "I'll read you *two*."
But now she's up to four.
Her eyes are getting bleary,
then she hears a tiny

SNORE.

We circle in amazement.

"Could he really be asleep?"

Mama eyes us sternly.

Whispers, "Shhhhh. Don't make a peep."

We watch him softly breathing,

lying snug on Mama's chest.

At last, the house is quiet.
At last, we get to rest.

Finally Mama rises,
laying Henry in his bed.
Then we gently—oh so gently—
kiss his sleepy little head.

"I'm exhausted," Mama murmurs,
as we tiptoe through the door.

But halfway down the hall,
she stops—
and Mama whispers:

MORE!